This book belongs to...

_____

© Illus. Dr. Seuss 1957

WACKY WEDNESDAY

By Theo. LeSieg

Illustrated by George Booth

ISBN 9-999-18656-4

Printed in Melrose Park, Illinois, U.S.A.

SP20000983JUL2016

WACKY WEDNESDAY

By Theo. LeSieg
Illustrated by George Booth

BEGINNER BOOKS   A Division of Random House, Inc.

It all began
with that shoe on the wall.
A shoe on a wall . . . ?
Shouldn't be there at all!

Then I
looked up.
And I said,
"Oh, MAN!"

And that's how
Wacky Wednesday
began.

I looked out
the window.
And I said,
"GEE!"

More things were wacky!
And I saw three.

I went
down the hall
and I said,
"HEY!"

Three
more things
were wacky today!

In the
bathroom,
MORE!

In the
bathroom,
FOUR!

I began to dress.
Then I said,
"WOW!"

Four MORE things
were wacky now!

I looked
in the kitchen.
I said,
"By cracky!
Five more things
are very wacky!"

I was late for school.

I started along.

And I saw that

six more things were wrong.

And then seven more!

And the Sutherland sisters!
They looked wacky, too.

They said,
"Nothing is wacky
around here but you!"

"But look!" I yelled.
"Eight things are wrong
here at school."

"Nothing is wrong,"
they said.
"Don't be a fool."

I ran into school.

I yelled to Miss Bass . . .

$2+3=5$

GEORGE WASHINGTON

... "Look!
Nine things
are wacky
right here
in your class!"

"Nothing is wacky
here in my class!
Get out!
You're the wacky one!
OUT!"
said Miss Bass.

I went out

the school door.

Things were worse than before.

I couldn't believe it.

Ten wacky things more!

Then I
counted
ELEVEN!

Then . . .
twelve WORSE things!
I got scared.
And I ran.

I ran
and knocked over
Patrolman McGann.

"I'm sorry, Patrolman."

That's all I could say.

"Don't be sorry," he smiled.

"It's that kind of a day.

But be glad!

Wacky Wednesday

will soon go away!"

"Only twenty things more
will be wacky," he said.

"Just find them
and then
you can go
back to bed."

Wacky Wednesday was gone
when I counted them all.
And I even got rid
of that shoe on the wall.

I CAN READ IT ALL BY MYSELF

Beginner Books